For my parents

Thanks also to Alissa Imre Geis, Susan Fama, my friends at Storyopolis,
Sarah & Hunter Heller, Stacey Zarcoff, Fonda Snyder & Dawn Heinrichs,
Linsey Herman, and Kathy Davis for all their advice and encouragement

Book design by Sara Gillingham and Adam J. B. Lane.
Typeset in Ebola Kikwit.

The illustrations in this book were rendered in 3-D mixed media.
Manufactured in China.

Library of Congress Cataloging-in-Publication Data
Lane, Adam.
Monsters party all night long / by Adam Lane
p. cm.
Summary: Dracula is feeling sad and throws a truly wild party in order to meet new friends.
ISBN 0-8118-4304-1
[1. Monsters—Fiction. 2. Parties—Fiction. 3. Loneliness—Fiction. 4.Stories in rhyme.] I. Title.
PZ8.3.L27659Mo 2004
[E]—dc22
2003014122

Distributed in Canada by Raincoast Books
9050 Shaughnessy Street, Vancouver, British Columbia V6P 6E5

10 9 8 7 6 5 4 3 2 1

Chronicle Books LLC
85 Second Street, San Francisco, California 94105

www.chroniclekids.com

chronicle books · san francisco

MONSTERS PARTY
ALL NIGHT LONG

by Adam J.B. Lane

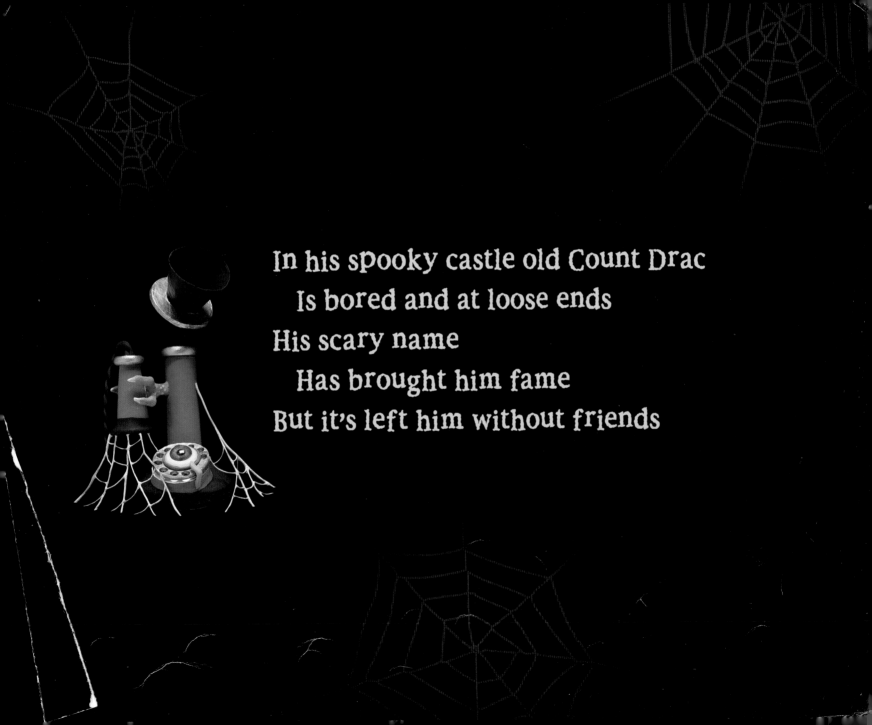

In his spooky castle old Count Drac
   Is bored and at loose ends
His scary name
   Has brought him fame
But it's left him without friends

Then an idea strikes the Count
   That gets him all excited
A party's how
   He'll make new pals
And everyone's invited!

From 'round the world to Castle Drac
   The monsters come a-knocking
And with a grin
   They're welcomed in
And soon the night is rocking

Down in the castle's dusty tombs
The creatures' toes are tapping
Deep underground
To the hip-hop sound
Of funky mummies rapping

Spinning out that ancient song
Monsters party all night long

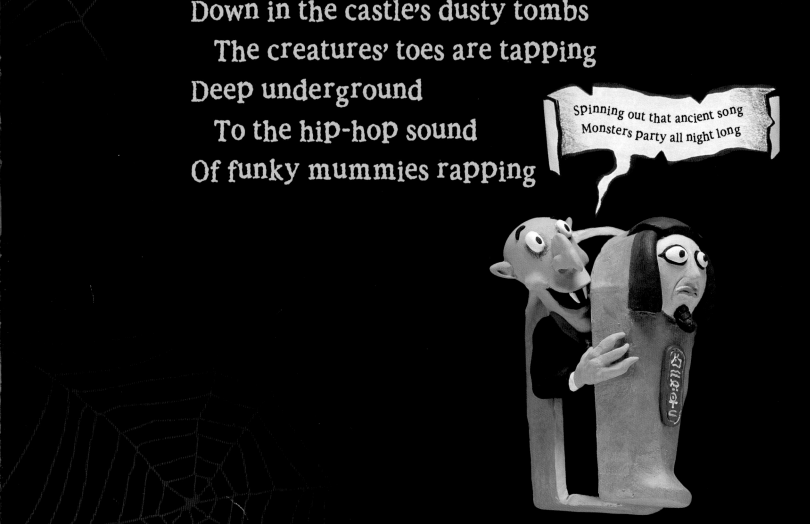

The Werewolf hits the dance floor
   To get in his disco groove
His chest's so hairy
   It's sorta scary
But his moves are pretty smooth

Shaking to that boogie song
Monsters party all night long

Sleep-'n-Stein has the flu
   And sadly can't attend
So his monster chums
   Are glad to come
And cheer up their sick friend

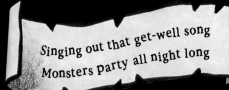

Singing out that get-well song
Monsters party all night long

Down in the nearby Bleak Lagoon
Upon the slimy sand
The Creature leads
The strings and reeds
Of his famous All-Fish Band

Dancing to that deep-sea song
Monsters party all night long

The zombies throw a fashion show
To flaunt the clothes they wear
They look real swell
Although they smell
And drop parts here and there

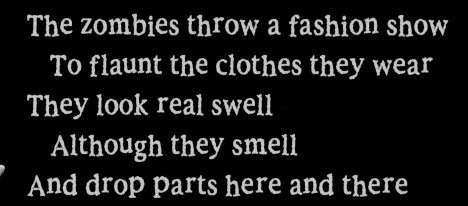

Strutting to that stylish song
Monsters party all night long

VOGRE

TERRIFIC
TALONS!

MONSTER
MAKEOVER

AND

FABULOUS
FANGS

SLIME
ITS BACK

NEW COFFINS
YOU'LL WANT TO BE CAUGHT DEAD IN

bone appétit!
toe jam on toast
eyeball puffs
french bunion soup
snot dogs
finger sandwiches
scab croquettes

For the hungry crowd Chef Boneapart
   Whips up some *horror d'oeuvres*
There's earwax chips
   And toenail tips
And scrambled brain preserves

Munching to that scrumptious song
Monsters party all night long

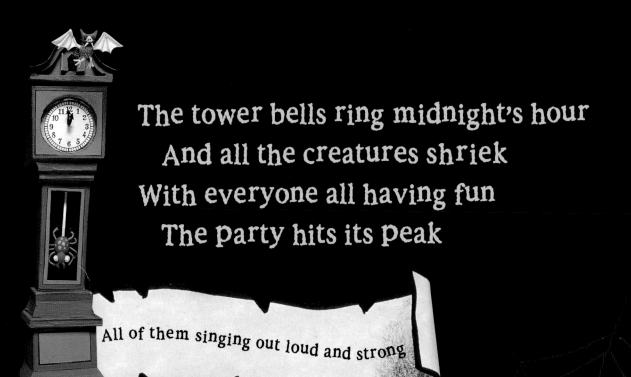

The tower bells ring midnight's hour
And all the creatures shriek
With everyone all having fun
The party hits its peak

All of them singing out loud and strong

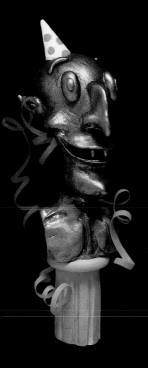

And Drac has learned a lesson
Now our story's reached its end:
Great wealth and fame
Just aren't the same
If they can't be shared with friends